300036

SCOOBY-DOO! and YOU:
A Collect the Clues Mystery
THE CASE OF THE CREEPY CAMP

By Jesse Leon McCann

WORLDWIDE PUBLISHING™

SCHOLASTIC INC.

New York   Toronto   London   Auckland   Sydney
Mexico City   New Delhi   Hong Kong

ISBN 0-439-23166-3

12 11 10 9 8 7 6 5 4 3 2   1 2 3 4 5/0

Cover and interior illustrations by Duendes del Sur
Cover and interior design by Madalina Stefan

Printed in the U.S.A.

First Scholastic printing, July 2001

All the new books you ordered have come in. You happily leave the bookstore with a bag full of novels to read. Images of wizards and broomsticks and kids who morph into animals fill your head. What could possibly make this day any better?

Then you see some friends going into the VeggieVu vegetarian restaurant next door. It's Scooby, Daphne, Fred, Velma, and Shaggy — the kids otherwise known as Mystery, Inc.!

"Hey, gang!" you holler. "Wait up!"

"Like, hey, look who's here!" Shaggy says with a smile.

Scooby-Doo runs up to you. "*Rello!*" he says with a grin.

"We were just about to have lunch," Velma explains. "Would you like to join us?"

"Sure!" you answer happily.

As the waitress seats you, Daphne whispers, "This is the best vegetarian restaurant in town. The food is so good that Scooby and Shaggy don't even notice there's no meat or dairy products in it."

Everything on the menu looks so good. You can't decide if you want the oriental salad or the tofu lasagna.

Scooby and Shaggy know exactly what they want. They don't even look at the menu.

"Six large pepperoni pizzas, please!" Shaggy says hungrily.

"*Reah, ree roo!*" Scooby grins.

You snicker to yourself. You know the pizza is delicious, even though the "pepperoni" and "cheese" is made of tofu. What

would Scooby and Shaggy think if they knew?

While you wait for your order, you ask what the gang has been up to.

"Oh, we just came back from solving a great mystery!" Fred says. "It happened while we were counselors at a summer camp. Would you like to hear about it?"

"Of course," you answer with a smile. Hearing about Scooby and the gang's mysteries is almost as exciting as reading about them!

"I'll bet you could have helped us solve it, if you'd been there," Velma comments.

At that moment, the waitress returns with the food. Oriental salad for you, spinach soufflé for Fred, spaghetti for Velma, tortilla soup for Daphne, and, of course, twelve pizzas for Shaggy and Scooby-Doo.

Before you can pour the dressing on your salad, you hear a symphony of munching, crunching and burping. Looking up, you watch with amazement as Scooby and Shaggy eat.

First, they both stick their pointing fingers up into the air and spin the pizzas. As the pizzas twirl, they chomp and chomp and chomp until the pizzas are gone. After repeating this maneuver a few times, all the pizzas are gone.

"Six more pizzas, please!" Shaggy calls to the waitress.

"*Rake rit a rozen!*" Scooby adds.

"Like, make it *two* dozen!" Shaggy laughs.

"After all, the afternoon is still young! Heh heh heh!"

With a smile and a knowing look, Daphne turns back to you.

"Anyway, we were telling you about our latest mystery," she says.

"Hey, I know!" Velma says with a smile. "We'll tell you the story of our campground case, and you can solve it!"

"That sounds like fun!" you say.

"I've even got something to help you," Daphne says as she holds up a small wire-bound notebook. She hands the notebook

over to you. "It's our Clue Keeper. I took the notes this time. I wrote down everything that happened — the people we met, the clues we found, and anything else that seemed important. We call this one *The Case of the Creepy Camp*."

"All you have to do is read the Clue Keeper," Velma says. "We've even added some shortcuts. Whenever you see this 👁👁 , you'll know you've met a suspect in the case. And whenever you see this 🔦 , you've found a clue."

"Our Clue Keeper is divided into sections," Fred adds. "At the end of each section, we'll help you organize the things you've found. All you'll need is your own Clue Keeper and a pen or pencil."

The waitress returns with more pizzas for Shaggy and Scooby. Once more the spinning begins.

But you're too excited to watch them. You want to know all about the mystery.

"All right then," Daphne says, pointing to the Mystery, Inc. Clue Keeper. "Just open it up and begin with Clue Keeper entry number one of *The Case of the Creepy Camp.*"

Eagerly, you begin to read.

Clue Keeper Entry 1

The Mystery Machine climbed the thin, winding road toward the top of the tree-covered mountain.

"I'm so excited!" I said. "What a great opportunity for us to be camp counselors this summer! There will be all sorts of sports and activities: hiking, swimming, biking, and rock climbing! I can't wait to get there."

"Like, me neither, Daphne." Shaggy looked at me with a white face. "But if we don't stop all these twists and turns, I might lose my lunch!"

"*Rurp!*" added Scooby. "*Reah, ree, too!*"

"Maybe if you both hadn't eaten a whole carton of double-chocolate-stuffed marsh-mallow graham-cracker pies for lunch — especially before going up a winding road — you might not be in danger of losing it!" Velma said with a frown.

"Don't worry, gang," Fred said, smiling. "We're almost there."

"Like, what's the name of this camp, any-way?" Shaggy asked, taking deep breaths.

"Camp Mystery Peak," I answered. "That's the name of this mountain, 'Mystery Peak.' And it's at the very top of this moun-tain."

Scooby got a sudden look of fear in his eyes, momentarily replacing the look of nau-sea. "*Rystery Reak? Rulp!*"

"Mystery? That's fitting for us," Velma said. "Why do they call it that?"

I read from a brochure the camp had sent

us: "According to this, there's legend about strange happenings on this mountain.

"Eerie wood sprites have been encountered over the years," I continued. "Many have reported seeing these angry creatures, described as five feet tall, being part-man, and part-tree, with weird, glowing eyes!"

"Z-z-zoinks!" cried Shaggy. "P-p-part tree?"

"*Reird, rowing ryes?*" Scooby shuddered.

If possible, they both looked sicker than before.

"Anyway, that's just a myth," I said. "There's no such thing as wood sprites."

"Here's the campground!" Fred announced. He pulled the Mystery Machine into a parking space, and we all piled out.

A young man and woman came to greet us. They were wearing Camp Mystery Peak T-shirts. They didn't look very happy.

"You must be the rest of the counselors," the boy said, frowning. "I'm Mike Ridgway, and this is my sister, Paula. We're the head counselors."

10

"What's the matter?" Fred asked. "You don't seem very happy to see us."

"Oh, it's not you," Paula said. "We just don't like being here, that's all."

"You see, our father owns this camp," Mike explained. "Every summer he makes us come up here and run the place. We're sick of it."

"Yeah," agreed Paula. Mike and Paula led us to our cabins, then excused themselves, saying they had to gather firewood. Meanwhile, Shaggy and Scooby unloaded our gear from the Mystery Machine.

"We've got two days before the campers get here," I explained. "That will give us time to get squared away and get to know the area."

"This is going to be fun!" Fred smiled. "Even though it's a summer job it will seem more like a vacation. I don't mind getting away from mysteries, ghoulies, and ghosts for a while!"

Suddenly, there came a screaming from

12

outside! We ran to investigate — and couldn't believe what we saw!

Out of the woods came a creature. It looked like a small man, but it also looked sort of like a tree!

Instead of arms and hands, it had gnarled tree branches that ended in prickly claws. Instead of feet, it had tangled roots. Worst of all, it had angry, glowing eyes!

Shaggy and Scooby screamed as the wood sprite chased after them.

"*Grrrowl!*" it roared.

I looked at Fred. "You were saying something about a vacation?"

Velma's Mystery-Solving Tips

*"J*inkies! I bet you can't wait to find out what happened next. First you have to make an entry in your Clue Keeper. Did you see the on page 10? That's your tip that you've found your first suspects. Now answer the questions below."

1. Who are the suspects in this entry?

2. Why are they at Camp Mystery Peak?

3. Why would they want the camp closed down?

14

Clue Keeper Entry 2

Eyes glowing with menace, the wood sprite chased Scooby and Shaggy around the camp's swimming pool and through the baseball field. It wasn't very fast, or very big, but it looked strong and fierce.

It was wearing old camper's clothing. Its wool shirt and jeans were rotting so much, there were holes in them. Through the holes, all that could be seen were tangles of tree branches. Its beard and hair were tufts of wild green moss.

"Like, help!" Shaggy cried. "I think this ungroovy ghoul's bark is as bad as its bite!"

"*Relp! Relp!*" Scooby yelled.

"In here!" Fred called, motioning for them to join us in a cabin.

As quick as a wink, Shaggy and Scooby ran through the field and were inside the cabin with us.

"Zoinks! Close the door, Fred!" Shaggy yelled. "Quick!"

Fred slammed the door shut just in time. The creature began to hammer on the door with thunderous blows.

"*Arrrowwwwwwwl!*" the creature growled.

"That's one angry spirit!" I said.

"Like, no fooling!" Shaggy was breathing hard.

"*Ruh-huh! Ruh-huh!*" Scooby-Doo agreed, nodding furiously.

Then there came more growls. "*Ooooooo!*" It was coming from the woods around the campground — from many different places!

"Jinkies!" Velma remarked. "It sounds like the whole forest is filled with them!"

Fred had the door open and was peeking through the crack. "Come on, the creature went back into the forest when the others started howling. It's time to do some investigating!"

"Like, I was afraid you were going to say that!" Shaggy groaned as Scooby whimpered.

As a group, we left the cabin and entered the forest in the direction the sprite had disappeared.

We made an extra effort to be as quiet as possible. This wasn't an easy thing to do, since we had to drag Scooby and Shaggy along all the way.

"Zoinks! I keep telling you guys, Scooby and I would be more than willing to stay back and guard the Mystery Machine — from the inside with the doors locked and the windows rolled up! Right, Scoob?"

"*Roo ret!*" Scooby peered all around the deep woods.

"Fat chance, boys," Velma said. "You're staying right with us."

It didn't take very long for us to find something interesting. We came to a small clearing between the tall trees.

"Look, gang!" Fred whispered.

In the clearing, completely out of place, was a big speaker like you might find attached to a stereo. The only difference was, there was no wire connecting it to anything. Instead, it had a small radio device and an antenna on top.

"I've seen one of these before," Fred com-

mented. "It's a battery-powered wireless speaker."

"What in the world is it doing out in this forest?" Velma asked.

"I'm not sure." Fred frowned, thinking hard. "Let's look around."

We found three more speakers, just like the first one. They were in various places. It was very puzzling.

"It will be dark soon," I said. "I think we should go back to camp and see if Mike and Paula can shed any light on this mystery."

"Man, I'm with you!" Shaggy said happily. "Besides, I hear these camps are well stocked with snacks! Scoob and I missed our late afternoon meal!"

"*Reah!*" Scooby smacked his lips.

With Shaggy and Scooby in the lead, we hiked back. We hadn't gone very far, however, when it happened.

Two figures jumped out from behind trees and grabbed Scooby and Shaggy. Their green, alien faces snarled, and their weird eyes at the end of long stalks blinked angrily.

"What are you doing here, human?" one of the aliens demanded.

Shaggy and Scooby did the only thing they *could* do — they fainted!

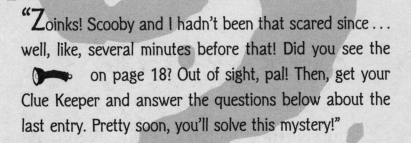

Shaggy and Scooby's Mystery-Solving Tips

"**Z**oinks! Scooby and I hadn't been that scared since . . . well, like, several minutes before that! Did you see the 🔦 on page 18? Out of sight, pal! Then, get your Clue Keeper and answer the questions below about the last entry. Pretty soon, you'll solve this mystery!"

1. What was the clue in the last entry?

2. What could the clue be used for?

3. What knowledge would a person have to have to use this clue?

Clue Keeper Entry 3

Of course, they weren't really aliens. As soon as Shaggy and Scooby hit the dirt, the two strangers took off their rubber masks.

"Wow! Are they okay?" the first stranger asked.

As we helped our friends up, the strangers introduced themselves.

"I'm Les," said the first one.

"I'm Wes. No relation," said the other.

Les was real skinny and wore thick glasses. Wes was short and round.

"We're counselors at Camp Gulch," said Les proudly.

"We didn't mean to scare you, but technically you're trespassing on Camp Gulch territory," said Wes. "It's our job to keep out enemy intruders."

The two pointed off into the woods. Sure enough, through the dusky gloom we could see the lights of another camp nestled nearby.

"Because you're heading in the direction of Camp Mystery Peak, we must assume you are our enemies!" Les declared.

"What do you mean?" I asked.

"Camp Gulch is a science camp," Wes explained. "Since your camp is sports related, our two camps don't get along."

"In other words, every year the guys from your camp pick on the guys from our camp." Les looked sad, yet he shrugged. "They call us nerds. That's okay, we're used to it."

"Well, that's nonsense!" Fred said. "We

like science, too. We use it often in our detective work."

"It doesn't matter," Les said gloomily. "Even if you counselors don't pick on us, your campers will pick on our campers. Sometimes I wish they hadn't ever built another camp around here. It was so peaceful before Camp Mystery Peak came along."

We tried to assure them that this year it would be different. But Les and Wes weren't convinced. After years of being made fun of, it was hard to believe things were going to change.

They didn't know anything about the speakers in the forest or wood sprites when

we asked them. Since it was getting dark really fast, we decided to depart.

Back at our camp, we met up with Mike and Paula Ridgway in the dining hall. Everyone had to eat cold sandwiches, they informed us, since they couldn't figure out how to start the oven.

It didn't matter to Shaggy and Scooby. They gobbled down a stack of sandwiches each, while we told the Ridgways about seeing the wood sprite. They looked at each other as if we were crazy.

"Didn't you hear all the howling in the woods?" Velma asked. "It was really loud."

"We didn't hear a thing," Paula replied. "We were on the other side of the peak practicing our rock climbing."

The Ridgways changed the subject and told us how they loved rock climbing. They wanted to go climbing in the Grand Tetons that year, but their father made them come take care of the camp, as usual.

We told them about what Les and Wes had told us. They just shook their heads and laughed hard. They called the Camp Gulch counselors a couple of goofy guys.

By then, it was really late and it was time to turn in. We said our good nights and began our hike back to our cabins. It was really dark outside, since the moon hadn't risen. We all carried flashlights.

About halfway to the cabins, I began to fall behind. My flashlight kept blinking out. I had to smack it to get it working again. It wasn't long before the others were way ahead of me.

"Hey, you guys!" I called. "Wait up!"

I started to walk faster. Then my light went out again and I couldn't get it to come

26

back on. I tried to hurry after the rest of the gang, following the glow of their flashlights. But before I knew it, I stumbled over something and fell to the ground.

Suddenly, I got the feeling that I wasn't alone.

"Fred? Velma? Shaggy?" I asked weakly. "Scooby-Doo, is that you?"

Something moved in the darkness. I was startled to realize a figure was standing right in front of me!

Then the figure let loose with a shrill, crazy laugh. "*Hoo hoo hoo!* What's the matter, girlie? Lose your way?"

Fred's Mystery-Solving Tips

"Boy, I'll bet you're wondering who Daphne met! We'll get back to the story in a moment. But first, jot down the suspects found in the last chapter. Did you see the on page 22? Great! Grab your Clue Keeper and answer the questions below."

1. Who were the suspects found in the last entry?

2. What are these suspects doing in the forest?

3. Is there a reason these suspects would want Camp Mystery Peak closed? What is it?

Clue Keeper Entry 4

"What do you want?" I asked as I stumbled to my feet. "Who are you?"

"Why, girlie, I'm just old Mr. Codger! This here is my mountain," the man said. Then he laughed again. "*Hoo! Hoo!* Here, let me light my flashlight."

Suddenly, his flashlight lit up and I could see him clearly.

Mr. Codger was a short old fellow with red cheeks and a shiny nose. He smiled up at me warmly.

"There, now! That's better, eh, girlie?" He grinned.

"Yes, much," I said. "Thank you, Mr. Codger."

Just then, the rest of the gang came back looking for me.

"Like, Daphne I'm so glad you're okay!" Shaggy exclaimed.

"We were afraid something terrible had happened!" Velma said.

"I'm okay now," I told them. "Mr. Codger helped me."

"Glad to do it! *Hoo! Hoo!*" Mr. Codger remarked happily, and shook hands all around.

"Gee, Mr. Codger, maybe you can help us clear up this mystery," Fred inquired. "What can you tell us about the wood sprites?"

Mr. Codger's cheerful face took on a dreadfully serious look, "Ah, you don't want to be messing with them, kids! Them sprites are mighty dangerous!"

"*Rangerous?*" Scooby said and gulped.

"You bet!" Mr. Codger told us. "I own the land on this mountain but I wish I'd never seen it. Many a hiker's disappeared into the woods, and ain't never been heard from again! Jealous, sprites are. Jealous of this mountain! With hearts as black and as evil as a rotten tree! If they had their way, wouldn't be a human left on Mystery Peak come morning!"

"Zoinks! Why wait till morning?" Shaggy gasped. "Let's leave now!"

Fred smiled. "Not until we figure out what's going on here. Mr. Codger, do you own the camps on this mountain, too?"

"No, sir, sonny. The camp owners pay me

rent to use the land. I wish they'd close them camps down. It ain't safe."

"Thanks for the information, Mr. Codger," I said. "Can we walk you home?"

"Ah, no thanks, girlie!" Mr. Codger looked happy again. "I live way down on the other side of the peak. *Hoo!* And my poor old knees ain't good for walking much any more. I have an all-terrain vehicle parked over by the tennis courts!"

With that, Mr. Codger waved good-bye and walked into the night

Soon after, Velma and I were in our cabin, and the boys were in theirs. We were glad to be inside, in our beds, about to snuggle into our sleeping bags.

And just as we were about to go to sleep . . .

Knock! Knock! Knock! Someone knocked on our door.

Velma and I were wide awake again. We quietly crept to the door, barely breathing.

"Who is it?" I demanded.

"It's Shaggy," came the reply.

Sighing, I opened the door.

"Like, hi, Daphne." Shaggy grinned, stumbling in. "I forgot to get my bedtime Scooby Snacks from you."

I couldn't help but smile. "Yes, heaven forbid you'd have to go to sleep on an empty stomach!"

I gave Shaggy a handful of Scooby Snacks. He sat down on the floor and started to munch the snacks . . . a little too loudly.

"Shaggy, do you mind?" I complained. "I want to get my beauty sleep!"

"Like, sorry, Daph!" Shaggy said, and he covered his mouth with his hands to muffle the crunching.

At that point . . .

Tap! Tap! Tap! Someone tapped on the door.

Grumbling, Velma got back out of bed and answered it.

"*Ri, Relma!*" Of course, it was Scooby-Doo. "*Redtime Rooby Racks?*"

Velma climbed back in her bunk as the two of them sat snacking in the corner. Velma groaned and put her pillow over her head. Shaggy whispered to Scooby and they both continued chewing more quietly.

And then . . .

Knock! Knock! Knock!

Now Velma was getting annoyed. She jumped out of her bunk and stomped to the door. Throwing it open, she exclaimed, "Fred, I can't believe you want Scooby Snacks, too!"

But it wasn't Fred.

Daphne's Mystery-Solving Tips

"*J*eepers! Things are pretty exciting now, huh? We'll get back to the story in a minute. But first, did you see the 👀 on page 29? He could be an important suspect. Open your Clue Keeper and answer the questions below."

1. What suspect was introduced in this entry?

2. What is this suspect's connection with Mystery Peak?

3. What did you learn about this suspect's hobby?

Clue Keeper Entry 5

The wood sprite charged into our cabin th an angry roar! Its sinister, glowing eyes d. Its branchlike fingers grabbed for stench from its mossy beard and hing was almost overpowering.

" it howled, and several an- uld be heard outside.

36

Around and around and around the inside of the cabin it chased us. It moved with a stiff-legged gait that reminded me of a walking tree — or of a Frankenstein's monster!

We all raced out the door, with the growling creature hot on our tails. Outside, the other howling wood sprites screamed from inside the woods. We couldn't see them, but their howls told us they were there, all right!

"Zoinks! I think he's trying to chase us toward his creepy cousins!" Shaggy cried.

"*Reah! Reepy rousins!*" Shaggy whimpered.

"We'd better stay away from the thick part of the forest." I pointed to an area past the basketball court where the trees were few and far between.

The moon was up now and lit our way. This was a good thing because we didn't have our flashlights.

"*Hooorrrrooooowl!*"

We left the campground, scrambling over picnic tables and around trees. The sprite ran after us, wailing angrily all the way.

I peeked over my shoulder. The other sprites didn't appear to be following. Their shrieks died down as we crossed over the mountain's summit and descended the other side.

Then we stopped. We had to.

We'd come to a dead end. The ground just

suddenly dropped away. We were now standing on the edge of a rock cliff. Looking down,
we could tell we were about fifty feet up.

"Now what do we do?" I exclaimed.

"*Hooooowrrrrrul!*" the sprite yowled
wildly. It knew it had us trapped!

Clue Keeper Entry 6

Then I spotted our way out!

"Look!" I pointed to the edge of the cliff.

Someone had left two neatly coiled ropes attached to spikes driven into the rock there.

"I'll bet those belong to Mike and Paula," Velma exclaimed. "They must come here to practice their rock climbing!"

"Right!" I agreed. "And lucky for us, we've also learned rock climbing! Let's go!"

Rappelling down the side of a rock face isn't easy. It's even harder without gloves. You have to go slowly to prevent friction burns from the rope. And, boy! Do your legs get a workout!

Nevertheless, we did pretty well. We were about three-quarters of the way down, when Velma turned to me. "Daphne, do you have any idea if wood sprites can climb down ropes?" she asked.

I had to admit that I didn't know. When we'd all reached the bottom, I looked up. I fully expected to see the angry ghoul following right behind us. But it was still at the top, walking back and forth along the edge. It looked furious!

And as it waved its prickly claws at us and growled, a white piece of paper fell out the pocket of its moldy shirt. I grabbed for it, but missed. The paper fluttered down toward us. This seemed to anger it even more. It howled and jumped up and down like it was going to burst with exasperation.

Then, finally, it stalked away and we could no longer hear or see it.

I caught the piece of paper and held it up in the moonlight. It appeared to be a map of some sort. But I didn't get a good look at it, because suddenly a big shadow fell over us.

Something had jumped out from behind a rock. "Bwah-hah-hah-hah-haaaa!" it laughed shrilly.

"Very funny, Fred," I said drily, my hand on my hip. "We all knew it was you."

When Fred heard all the commotion back

at the campground, he'd tried following us. He must have taken the wrong turn, because he lost our tracks. By a stroke of luck, he managed to find us at the bottom of the cliff.

Back together again, Fred, Velma, and I looked at the map. It appeared to be a drawing of where Camp Mystery Peak stood. But the campground was gone, and in its place was a big building labeled THE LODGE.

We studied the map more closely. The slopes running downhill from the peak were labeled RUN #1, RUN #2, and RUN #3. Also,

there were areas marked as POSSIBLE LIFT ROUTE and SNOW-MAKING MACHINE LOCATION.

"What do you think it means?" I asked.

"I'm not sure," Fred pondered. "C'mon, gang, let's get back to our cabins."

Since we didn't want to climb back up the rock cliff and possibly run into the creatures, we circled around through the woods. After a bit, the trees grew closer together. The branches blocked most of the moonlight. As minutes passed, it got darker. The darker it got, the more nervous we got.

Then, suddenly . . . . *snap! Whoosh!* . . . and, again . . . *snap! Whoosh!*

Someone — or something — grabbed Fred and Shaggy by their feet and lifted them up into the trees!

"We've got you now!" said a voice in the darkness.

Velma's Mystery-Solving Tips

"Wow! That was a big surprise, let me tell you! And, did you see the on page 43? Terrific! Now, take your Clue Keeper and write down your answers to the questions below."

 What clue was discovered in this entry?

 What is it used for? Is there anything strange about it?

3. Who might have use for something like this clue?

Clue Keeper Entry 7

At first it was shocking to see Fred and Shaggy hanging upside down from the trees. Then, after the initial surprise wore off, it looked sort of funny.

Velma and I started giggling. We couldn't help ourselves.

"*Ree hee hee!*" Even Scooby joined in.

We stifled our laughter as Wes and Les jumped out of the trees.

"Oh, it's you guys again," said Les.

It seems we had wandered too close to Camp Gulch a second time, and had fallen into one of Les and Wes's traps. That is, Shaggy and Fred had, as they hung by ropes tied to their feet.

"What do you think you're doing?" asked Wes.

"Like, you know, hanging around," said Shaggy as he tried to shake himself free.

All he did was shake free the goodies he'd stuffed in his pockets. Candy, chips, and cheese all hit the ground. In a heartbeat, Scooby was there, gobbling up the food.

"Zoinks! I was saving those for my midnight snack!" Shaggy cried.

This set us off laughing again.

Fred and Shaggy were set free and the Camp Gulch counselors questioned us.

"We knew you were up to something!" accused Wes. "Thought we wouldn't notice you sneaking up on us, eh?"

Velma explained what had happened. "But what about all the tire tracks?" asked Les. "Are you saying you didn't make them?"

"What tire tracks?" I said. "Can you show them to us?"

The pair led us a few hundred yards away to a clearing in the woods. There was another of the radio-controlled speakers. And running on the ground next to it were three fresh tire marks.

"We figure three people came through here on three motorbikes and set up these speakers all over this part of the woods," Les explained. "But if it wasn't you, somebody else is out here."

"We should get back to guard duty." Wes pointed up the mountain. "Your camp is in that direction. I wouldn't come back this way again, because we've set up dozens of traps in this area."

They disappeared back up into the trees, and we started hiking up the mountain.

"I'm starting to get an idea of what's going on around here," Velma said.

"Me, too," agreed Fred. "But we're going to need a plan. Let's get back to our cabins and have a pow-wow!"

Shaggy and Scooby's Mystery-Solving Tips

"Like, did you notice the far-out clue on page 48? Cool, man! It's a really important clue! Make sure you answer all the questions below in your Clue Keeper."

1. What was the clue you discovered in this entry?

2. Why do you think this clue was in that part of the woods?

3. What kind of thing could make this clue?

Clue Keeper Entry 8

"Like, are you sure this is absolutely necessary, Fred?" Shaggy moaned.

"*Reah,*" Scooby complained. "*I reel roolish!*"

"That's okay," Velma said with a smile. "You both look pretty foolish, too."

Using brown and green paint and some old clothes, we'd made Shaggy and Scooby into wood sprites. Actually, they weren't as scary as the real wood sprite. In fact, they looked downright silly.

"That does it! We're out of here!" cried Shaggy. "Like, it's bad enough we have to act as bait for a walking knotty pine, but to do it and get bad fashion reviews — well, it's too much!"

"Ruh-huh! Ruh-huh!" Scooby scowled. *"Roo ruch!"*

"Aw, c'mon, you guys! We need you to lure that creature," Fred insisted and then grinned. "And what better way to catch a sprite than with a couple more sprites?"

"Well, we're not doing it!" Shaggy started taking off his disguise. "We refuse!"

Scooby stood proud. *"Right! Ree reruse!"*

Velma gave a knowing smile, then turned to Shaggy and Scooby. "Will you do it for some Scooby Snacks?" she asked.

Scooby and Shaggy turned to her eagerly.

"Eh, like, how many Scooby Snacks, Velma?" Shaggy inquired.

Later, after the fee of three Scooby Snacks each had been paid, Shaggy and Scooby entered the woods. They wore the sprite disguises and walked with a stiff-legged gait, like the real sprite did.

Meanwhile, we hid deeper in the forest, waiting for the action to begin. It didn't take long.

The boys were making a lot of noise, like we'd instructed them to.

"You know what I hate most about being part tree?" Shaggy said loudly. "It's the way dogs treat us!"

"*Ruh?*" Scooby looked at him with an odd expression.

Suddenly, the howling began. It was as if there were dozens of wood sprites in the surrounding trees. Shaggy and Scooby stopped in their tracks and began to shake.

"L-l-like, don't be afraid, woodland brothers!" he called to them. "It's just us, two of your sprightly sprite buddies come to shoot the breeze!"

And then, the real wood sprite jumped out right in front of them. It growled horribly and its eyes glowed with piercing fury.

"*Haaarrrughhh!*"

"Then again, maybe we should make like a tree and leave!" Shaggy cried. "C'mon, Scoob!"

They ran. Sure enough, the sprite followed right behind, trying to grab them with its gnarly, prickly claws.

Then, when they'd reached the spot we had decided on, Shaggy and Scooby raced ahead of the creature. They jumped into the foliage and sat perfectly still. Just as we figured, their costumes acted like camouflage. The sprite passed right by them and continued downhill.

We caught up with Shaggy and Scooby. Then we waited. A moment later, we heard the sounds we were waiting for.

Snap! Whoosh!

And, then . . .

"Help! Somebody help me! I'm trapped!"

We followed the sound and soon came upon the wood sprite. It hung upside down, caught in one of Camp Gulch's traps.

"That worked like a charm," Fred said as he reached up and pulled at the sprite's mask. "Now, let's see who you are!"

"And that's how we solved *The Case of the Creepy Camp*," Shaggy says, grinning. "Now where's that waitress with more pizzas?"

Daphne winks and smiles at you. Then she turns to Scooby and Shaggy. "I'm surprised you two like the food here," she says slyly. "After all, it's not your usual fare."

"Why?" asks Shaggy. "Like, because it's a vegetarian restaurant? Nah, we love this food!"

Scooby nods enthusiastically. *"Right! Ree rove rit!"*

Daphne is dumbfounded, "You mean you knew?"

"Sure, Daphne!" Shaggy says casually. "Scoob and I eat here all the time."

You chuckle to yourself as you turn to Velma and Fred.

"Well, now you've met all the suspects and found all the clues," Fred says. "Do you think you can solve the mystery?"

You smile and say you think you can.

"Terrific!" Velma says. "Here's some advice — look at your list of suspects and clues, then answer these questions.

"First, who do you think had a good reason to scare people away from Camp Mystery Peak?"

"Second, who do you think had the 'know-how' to scare people away from the camp?" Fred asks.

"Third, who do you think had the opportunity to scare people away from the camp?" Daphne asks.

"See if you can eliminate any of the suspects first," Velma suggests. "Then, using all of the information you've collected as well as your own smarts, try to figure who the wood sprite really was."

Daphne says, "Then when you think you've got it figured out, we'll tell you who was behind the mystery."

You start thinking very carefully.

Do you think you know who was behind The Case of the Creepy Camp? When you're ready to solve the mystery, turn the page.

59

"Mr. Codger was behind the wood sprite scare," Velma announces. "He wanted Camp Mystery Peak closed down, so he planned to scare all the campers away. Then he would have been able to build a winter ski attraction, which would make him a lot of money."

"So he dressed up like an angry Wood Sprite, and set up speakers all through the forest," Fred continues. "Whenever he'd appear, he'd run the sound of howling through the speakers to make it appear as if the woods were filled with creatures."

60

"And, like, it wasn't three people on three motorbikes setting up the speakers, like Les and Wes thought," Shaggy says. "It was one person — Mr. Codger — on a *three-wheeled* all-terrain vehicle."

"It couldn't have been Paula or Mike Ridgway. They couldn't even turn on an oven, so we knew they couldn't set up the speakers. Besides, either of them would have followed us down the ropes at the cliff, since they're both excellent rock climbers," Daphne says. "But Mr. Codger has bad knees and couldn't climb after us."

"And Mr. Codger's bad knees are why the wood sprite walked so stiffly," Fred says.

"Now, Wes and Les could have thought up the speaker idea," Shaggy adds. "But, like, we knew it wasn't them because they kept catching us and letting us go. If they were behind it, they would have dressed up as the wood sprites when they caught us, not as phony aliens."

All the gang is now looking at you.

"So, how did you do?" Daphne asks.

61

"I'll bet you solved the mystery like a pro!" Velma smiles. "You're a smart person, having read so many books."

"You know, it all turned out okay," Fred says with a grin.

"Come back and visit us again," Velma says. "There are always plenty of mysteries that need solving."

"And, like, we always like having company when we're spinning pizzas!" Shaggy says. "Right, Scoob, ol' pal?"

Scooby smiles. *"Rooby-rooby-roo!"* he shouts happily.